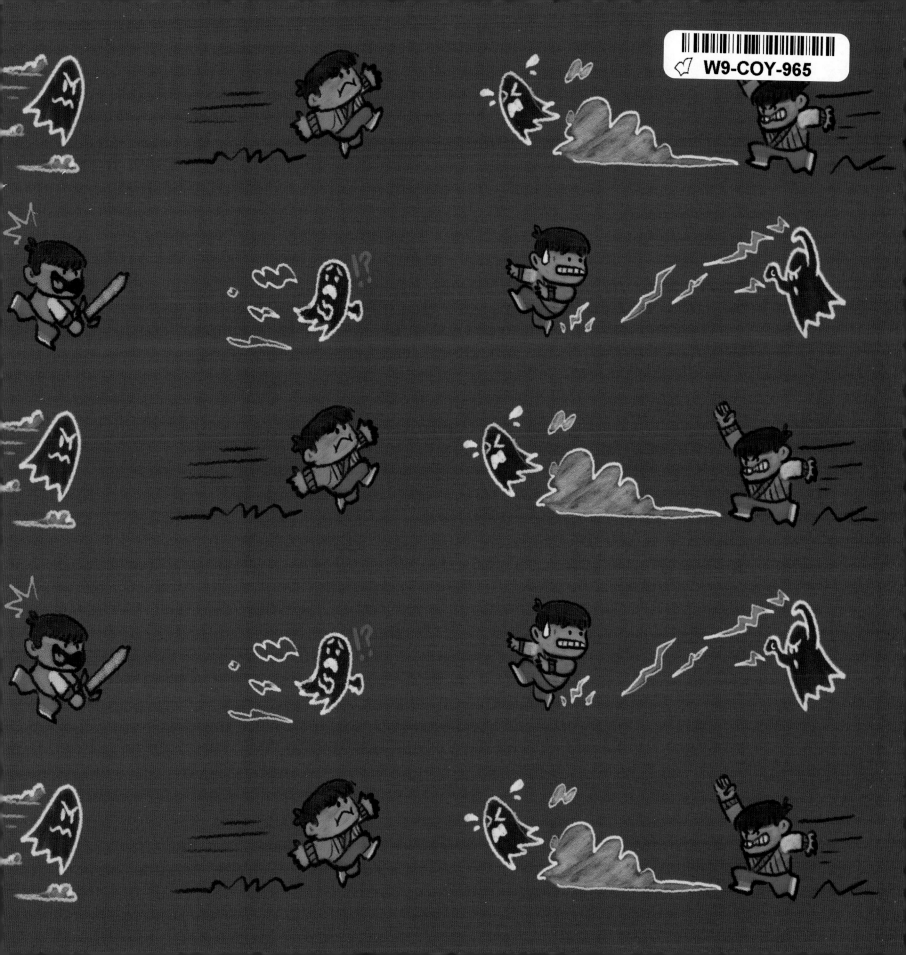

Bunso

Meets a

MUMU

Written & Illustrated by

Rev Valdez

"To my family,
who always encouraged me
to pursue my dreams."
—Rev

Hardcover 9781223186399
Paperback 9781223186405
Digital 9781223186412
Published by Paw Prints Publishing
PawPrintsPublishing.com
Printed in China

PAW PRINTS PUBLISHING

Glossary

Bunso (Boon-so) –
Youngest sibling or baby

Me

Big Meanie!

Blah Blah

Kuya (coo-yah) –
Elder brother or cousin

SCARY

Boo!

Ate (ah-tay) –
Elder sister or cousin

Who?

Mumu (Moo-Moo) –
????

Yikes!

mmmm...

Mumu loves dinuguan!

Dinuguan (Din-new-gwan) –
A stew made of pork blood, pork meat, chili and garlic

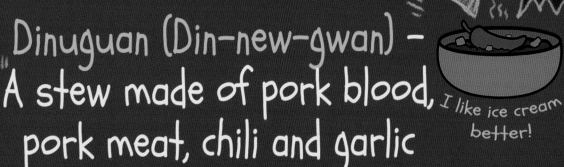

I like ice cream better!

My ^(ah-tay) Ate always tells me spooky stories at night, but the scariest one is about the ^(moo-moo) Mumu!

Not more stories!

She says the Mumu likes to punish kids who misbehave by sucking the fun outta everything!

My Kuya yelled: "Bunso, don't play my video games. If you do, the Mumu will get you!"

My Ate heard everything and she burst into laughter! "The Mumu has cursed you! You must have been really bad!"

The Mumu will not let me draw. The Mumu will not let me have ice cream. The Mumu will not even let me play video games!

The Mumu is taking away everything I love. If I don't stop him, who knows what will happen next?!

He told me . . .
"A Mumu is
a mad cow . . .
he attacks kids . . .
who stay up
too late!"

I asked my mom next and she said,

I asked my Kuya. He said,

uuu...Muu

Oh jeez!
It sounded sooooo scary!

But it is now or never!

I have to be BRAVE!

I will put an end to this once and for all!

I peek into the kitchen . . .

I imagine battling the Mumu

in all of its different forms.

I can't believe
I beat the Mumu!

But soon, I hear a noise . . .

It sounds like the Mumu is crying!

I feel sorry for him. It's risky,
but I want to take a peek.

He's round and soft,

like a marshmallow!

Turns out, he isn't the monster my family made him out to be.

The Mumu shows me his life story and how he got here.

It's been so long since he was alive,
he didn't know where to start.

He wants to try it all.

He did start to get
the hang of it.

Slowly.
Very slowly.

We were playing
my Kuya's games,

and before I knew it,
I dozed off!

It must have been past
the Mumu's bedtime too
because he left before I woke up!

My Mom made me clean all day!

It is worth it though

because I made
a new friend.

I grew up hearing wonderful stories full of Filipino folklore from my family, and have always felt a deep connection to mythology and storytelling. I was born in the Philippines, moved to San Francisco with my family when I was a small child, and I've been a Bay Area resident ever since. Art has been a huge part of my life, starting from my childhood when I watched my grandpa draw and marveled over his work. From him I gained a love of drawing, and it has helped to make me into the artist I am today. Whether it is drawing in pencil or on the computer, if I am creating art, I am a happy man. I love to read comic books and manga and am always down to watch a good scary movie. Family is one of my greatest inspirations and spending time with my siblings always brings a smile to my face, no matter what else is going on in the world. I hope you've enjoyed the world of Bunso as much as I have in creating it!

—Rev